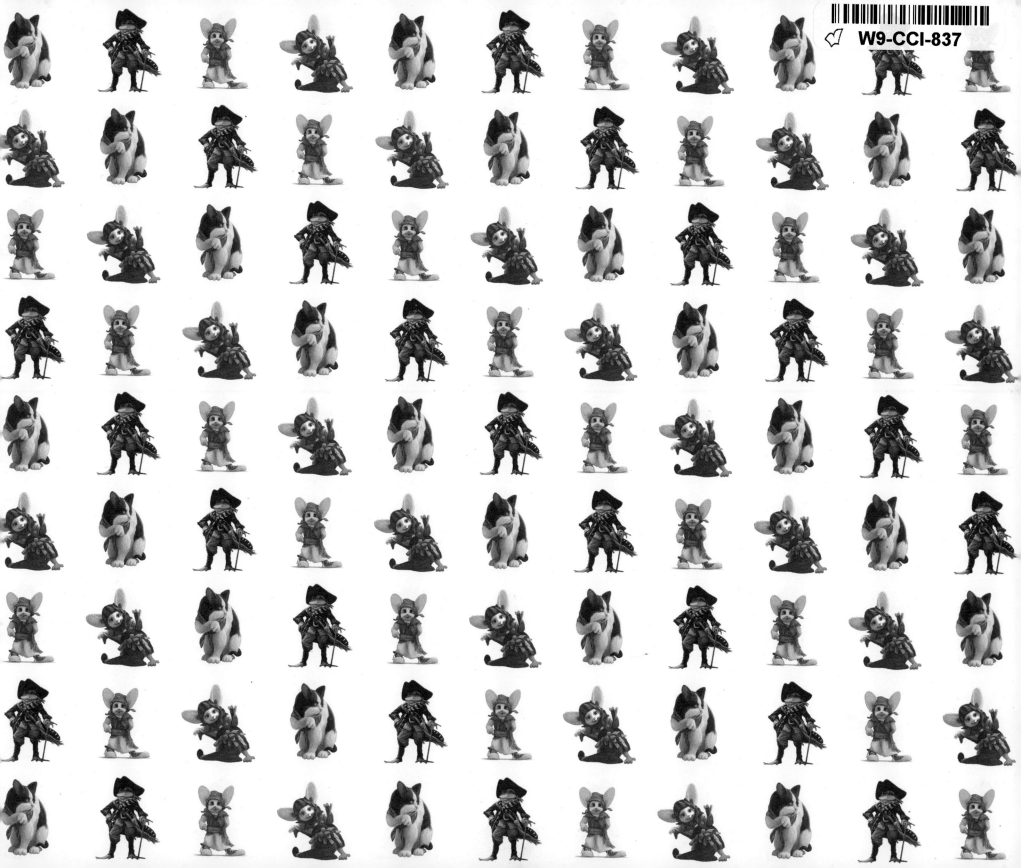

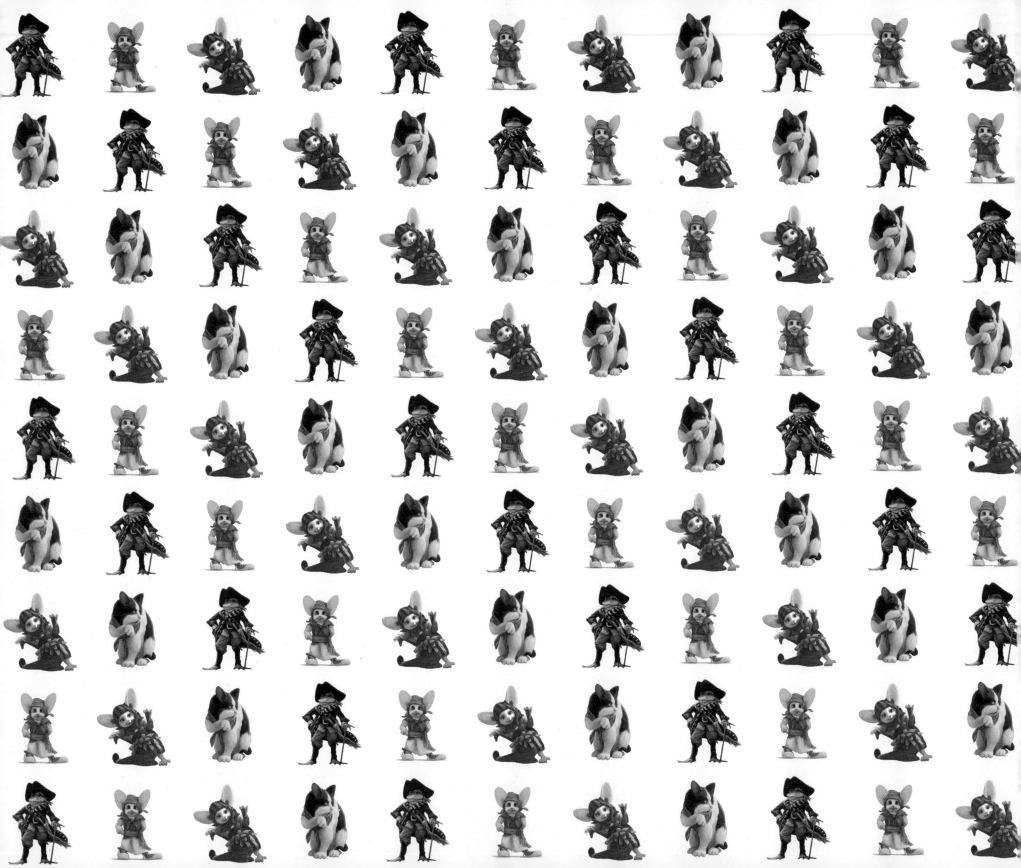

RIP SQUEAK AND FRIENDS

The Treasure

Written by **Susan Yost-Filgate**

Illustrated by **Leonard Filgate**

RIP SQUEAK, INC. ∾ SAN LUIS OBISPO, CALIFORNIA

To the memory of Harry, Jane, and Larry—
for teaching us that anything is possible.

PUBLISHED BY RIP SQUEAK, INC.
840 CAPITOLIO WAY, SUITE B
SAN LUIS OBISPO, CALIFORNIA 93405

LCCN: 2005926908

ISBN-13: 978-1-934960-41-7

Edited by Lee Cohen ∾ Designed by Willabel L. Tong

Don't miss the other books in this series:
rip squeak and his friends ∾ the treasure ∾ the adventure ∾ find the magic ∾ the surprise party

To learn more about other products from Rip Squeak, visit
www.RipSqueak.com

Printed in China
10 9 8 7 6 5 4 3 2 1
Revised Edition

Free activities for this book are available at www.raventreepress.com

RIP SQUEAK AND FRIENDS

The Treasure

Written by **Susan Yost-Filgate**

Illustrated by **Leonard Filgate**

Raven Tree Press
A Division of Delta Systems Co., Inc.
www.raventreepress.com

Rip Squeak looked out the window.
"Jesse, Abbey," he called to his sister and the kitten.
"Euripides is coming! Get ready for an adventure!"

Euripides was dressed in a
new costume.
"What's wrong?" Euripides
asked. "Haven't you seen a
pirate before?"

Euripides hopped onto the bed, dragging a big book behind him.
Rip, Jesse, and Abbey curled up together and listened as he read
stories about faraway places, pirates, and buried treasure.

When Euripides finished reading, a piece of paper fell out of his book.

"It's a treasure map!" Rip shouted.

Abbey looked closely. "What does the X mean?"

"X marks the spot!" said Euripides. "It's the place where pirates bury their treasure."

"A new adventure!" Jesse exclaimed.

"We must be properly dressed," said Euripides. They found colorful clothes in an old trunk and put them on.

"We look just like the pirates in Euripides' book!" said Rip. "Now we're ready to find that treasure."

Rip was ready to go, but Abbey was a little scared.
She wrinkled her nose and licked her fur.
"Don't worry," Rip smiled. "Your friends will protect you."

"Let's go," said Euripides. "The treasure is this way."

As they followed him into the woods, Euripides began to sing:

This thicket is full of creepy things,
With lots of eyes and legs and wings.
But we don't mind, it's such a pleasure
To work with friends to find the treasure!

When the friends stopped to rest, the map slipped out of Rip's hand. It fell into a deep hole.
"There it is!" said Abbey.
Rip reached down as far as he could. Then he heard someone yell!

"Watch out!" two ants hollered at him.

"Sorry," Rip said in a startled voice. "We need our map back. We have to find the treasure."

"Is it a treasure that you can eat?" asked one of the ants.

"No, but you are in luck," said Euripides. He pulled some cookies from his pocket.

"This *is* a treasure!" said the ant.

The ants happily crawled off.

"Now let's go find *our* treasure," said Jesse.

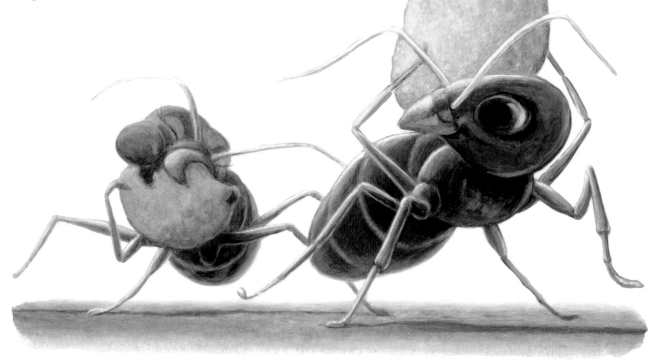

On their way they saw a mother duck with three babies.

"Where are you going?" Mother Duck asked.

"We're looking for treasure," Rip said politely.

"I have my treasure with me," said Mother Duck. "My children are my treasure."

"Gee," said Rip, "a treasure can be something different for each of us."

When they stopped to check the map, they heard a *buzzing* sound.

A strange creature hovered above them. His long, glowing wings never stopped moving.

"I should have known," Euripides smiled. "It's my friend, Dragonfly Sam."

Sam pointed to the X on the map. "I know where this is," said Sam, "but it's not exactly what I would call a treasure." Then he flew off.
"What did he mean by that?" asked Rip.
"We'll find out soon," replied Euripides.

The friends came to a small clearing.
"Wow!" they all shouted.
"It's just like the one in the book," said Jesse.
"Amazing," remarked Euripides.
"This really *is* a treasure!" Rip exclaimed.

Euripides hopped up on the
deck of the ship.
"It's a perfect day to set sail!"

"I feel like a real pirate," Rip said proudly. Euripides laughed. "This ship may not be important to everyone, but it's certainly a treasure to us."

Euripides raised the pirate flag. "I have a flag, too," said Jesse. She pulled out a scarf with a big, red heart on it. "I've never seen a pirate flag like that," said Euripides. "This flag will show everyone how we really feel," said Jesse. "You're right," Euripides grinned. "We'll fly both flags. We'll pretend we're real pirates, but everyone will know we're friendly."

"Prepare to sail!" shouted Euripides. A gentle breeze carried their pirate ship to open waters.

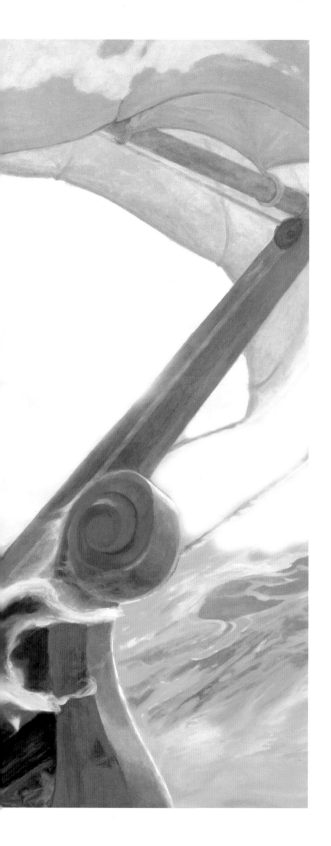

Rip Squeak couldn't wait for his next adventure. He knew he would be sharing it with the greatest treasure of all—his wonderful friends!

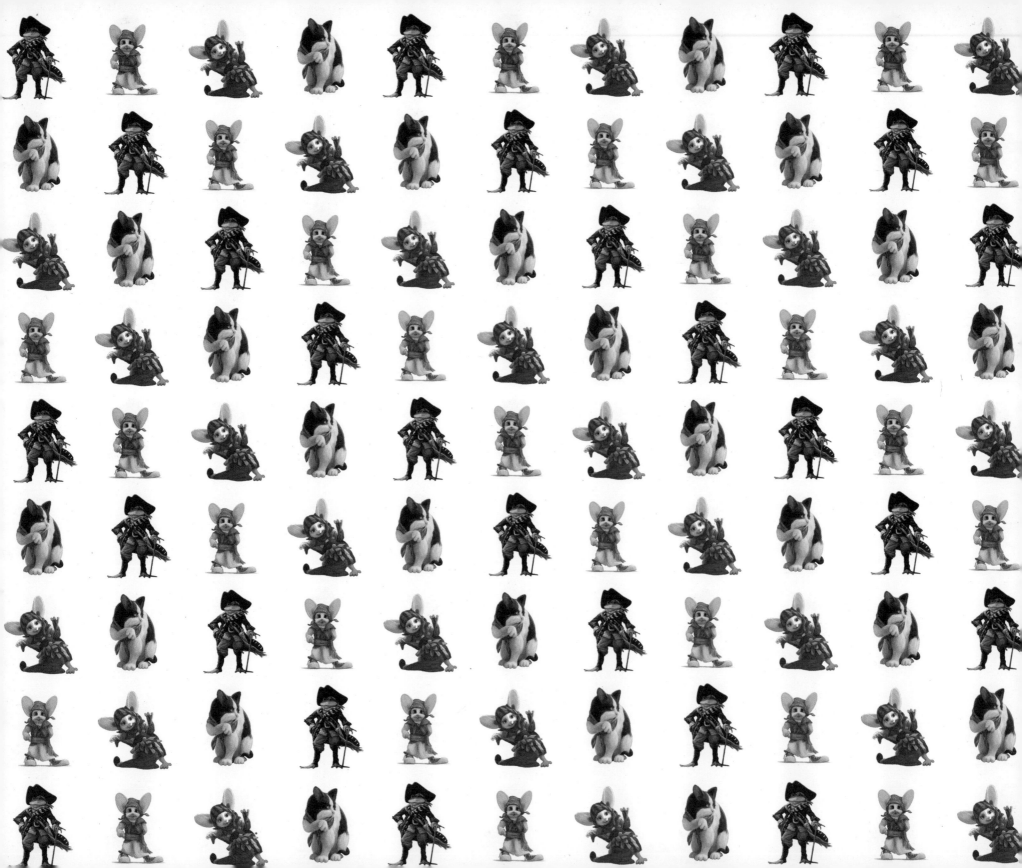